This Place IN THE Snow

REBECCA BOND

Dutton Children's Books ⌐ New York

CIP Data is available.

Published in the United States by Dutton Children's Books,
a division of Penguin Young Readers Group
345 Hudson Street, New York, New York 10014
www.penguin.com

Designed by Irene Vandervoort

Manufactured in China
First Edition
ISBN 0-525-47308-4

10 9 8 7 6 5 4 3 2 1

For my sister, who has always shared these places with me

A silent snow fell all night long.

It lay like lace along the trees.

It hatted the houses.

It capsuled the cars

in thick and sticky white.

A lumbering plow came rumbling, rattling, pushing up hillsides, up mountains, up snow,

rolling and rounding it, mounding it high
in creamy waves of white.

Now rooms asleep at once awakened.

And quiet turned noisy.

And noisy turned LOUD

with strings of cries and shrieks and shouts—

"The plow!"

"The plow!"

"The plow!"

And now came the flurry of dressing in woolens.

And there was the hurry of eating hotcakes.

And there was a hush as they stepped outside
to watch the work of the plow.

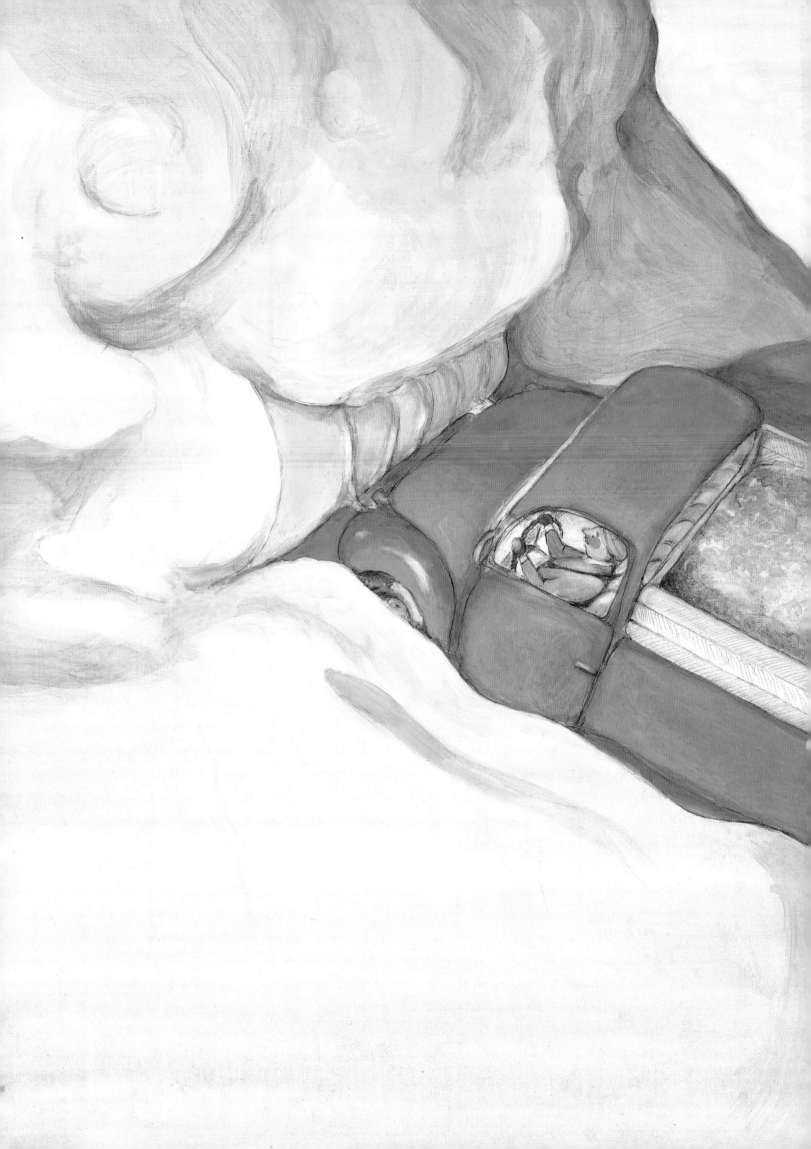

At last! With a wave, their snow mound was ready!

Like springs being sprung, they raced to the top.

And they looked down around them, at what this might be—
this place they would make in the snow.

And then came much talking and planning about it.

"Like this!" someone said.
"Or maybe like that!"
"And could we—"
"And we could—"
"And let's too—"
"Do THAT!"
They brightly, they greatly, agreed.

So now they began!

They tunneled.

They hollowed.

They tunneled deep pockets.

They hollowed large holes.

They shoveled great shovels, big spoonfuls of white,

sun-snow like lemon,

shade-snow light blue.

Then using their arms, they built up snow wallways.

And using their feet, they trampled snow floors.

They mounded snow spirals sky-high.

And using their might, they rolled and they rounded.

And after they finished their shaping

and carving

and shined things all shiny

and carefully swept,

together they felt it, just them . . .

and all this . . .

They were kings in a kingdom uncovered.

And though, much later, they went inside . . .

and took off wet snowsuits

and sat with hot soup,

that gauzy-white night,

they came out again
to the sound, in the town,
of the plow.

And they looked up there to the sky just above them.

And they looked down here to the ground just below.

And they looked all around them at what they could see—

This place, full of grace, in the snow.